D0101831

30131 05519579 3
LONDON BOROUGH OF BARNET

Everything was hot.

In memory of Tove Jansson, 1914-2001,
whose Moomintroll and friends started
a party in my imagination ~ S.T.

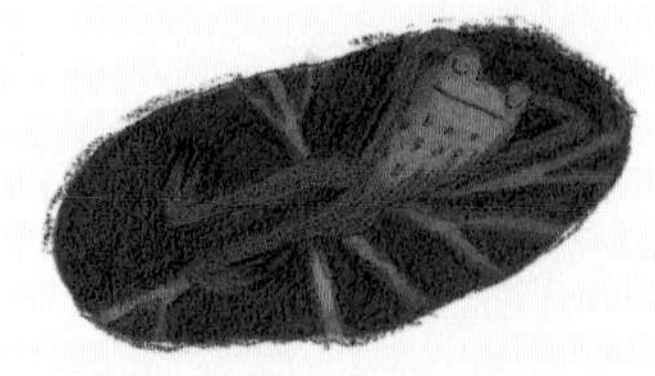

For Archer Kelly, who stirred my mind,
and gave me the courage to walk
on my own ~ E.H.

First published 2016 by Walker Books Ltd
87 Vauxhall Walk, London SE11 5HJ

2 4 6 8 10 9 7 5 3

This book has been typeset in Bembo

Printed in Malaysia

British Library Cataloguing in Publication Data:
a catalogue record for this book is available from the British Library

ISBN 978-1-4063-5132-3

www.walker.co.uk

A Brave Bear

illustrated by

SEAN TAYLOR **EMILY HUGHES**

WALKER BOOKS
AND SUBSIDIARIES
LONDON • BOSTON • SYDNEY • AUCKLAND

The sun was hot. The air was hot.
Even the shade was hot.

And my dad said, "I think a pair
of hot bears is probably the
hottest thing in the world."

But I thought up a good idea.
I said, "If we go to the river,
we can splash in and cool down!"

Dad said, "All right. Let's go then!"

It's quite a long way to get to the river.

There's the grassy part to go across.

Then the bushy part to push through.

After that, you've got to jump from rock to rock.

And I said, "I think a jumping bear is probably the jumpiest thing in the world!"

Dad told me, "Be careful.
Just do small jumps."

But I wanted him to see me do a big jump.
So I got myself ready.

I got myself steady...

And I slipped RIGHT OVER.

Dad helped me up.
But I was sad.
My knee was hurting.
Everything was too hot.

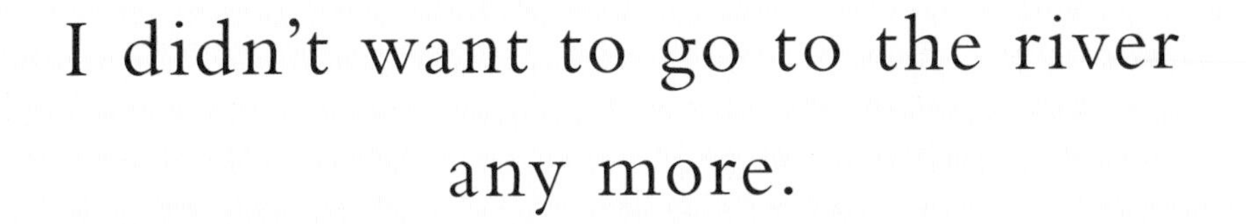

I didn't want to go to the river
any more.

Dad said we could wait for a bit.
And we both looked down at the water.

Then he said if I wanted to go on
he could give me a carry.

I like it when he gives
me a carry.

But I decided to go on my own.

And Dad said,
"I think a brave bear is probably
the bravest thing in the world!"

Down at the river,
Dad splashed in. I did, too.

We played about and cooled down.

And I said,
"I think a pair of wet bears
is probably the wettest thing
in the world!"

Even tomorrow was glowing.

On the way home, the sun was glowing.

The air was glowing...